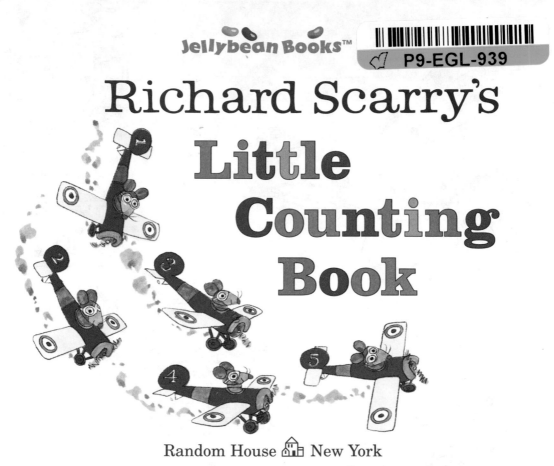

Richard Scarry's Little Counting Book

Random House 🏠 New York

Copyright © 1978 by Richard Scarry. All rights reserved. Originally published in different form in Great Britain as *Richard Scarry's Busy-Busy Counting Book* by William Collins Sons & Co. Ltd. Copyright © 1977 by William Collins Sons & Co. First published in the United States in 1978 by Random House, Inc. First Random House Jellybean Books™ edition, 1998. ISBN: 0-679-89238-9 http://www.randomhouse.com/

Printed in the United States of America   10 9 8 7 6 5 4 3 2 1

JELLYBEAN BOOKS is a trademark of Random House, Inc.

1 one

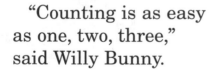

"Counting is as easy
as one, two, three,"
said Willy Bunny.

"Let's count all the things we see.
I will start with me. I am one bunny."

2 two

"Oh, look! Here comes Sally Bunny."

"One bunny and one bunny make
two bunnies."
   Both bunnies have two eyes, two hands,
two feet, and two long ears.

Willy and Sally go outside to play.
Along comes their friend Freddy Bunny.

Two bunnies and one bunny make
three bunnies.
How many wheels are on Freddy's tricycle?
That's right! There are three wheels.

 4 four

Here comes Flossie Bunny with her wagon.

Three bunnies and one bunny make
four bunnies.
  Now there are two girl bunnies and
two boy bunnies.
  Flossie has brought four apples in her
four-wheeled wagon for everyone to share.

5 five

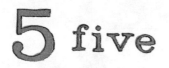

Then five race cars whiz by.
Can you count them?

"One, two, three, four, five," Willy counts.

6 six

Ding!
Ding!
Ding!
Ding!
Ding!
Ding!

Six fire engines
are speeding down the street.

7 seven

Willy sees seven cats
running past.

Five young cats, a mother,
and a baby cat make seven cats.

8 eight

How many places are set at the table? Eight.

There are five hot pies. And there are three cold pies.

How many pies are there? Eight.

9 nine

Willy sees nine firemen mopping the floor.

Five mops are red, two are green, and two are yellow.

How many mops are there? Nine.

10 ten

Here comes Father Cat with ten watermelons from his garden.

Five of the watermelons are safe in the basket. Five of the watermelons fly out.

The sixth, seventh, eighth, and
ninth watermelons are caught.

Will Mother Cat be able to catch
the tenth one before it falls to the ground?

Now let us see what we can count.

1

One Willy

2

Two bunnies

3

Three bunnies
and three trucks

4

Four buses

Five racing cars

6

Six fire engines

7

Seven cats

8

Eight pies

9

Nine mops

10

Ten watermelons!
And Mother Cat did catch
the last watermelon!

Can you add the
numbers the way Willy
has added them below
for his parents?

$1 + 1 = 2$

$2 + 1 = 3$

$2 + 2 = 4$

$3 + 2 = 5$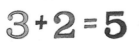

3 + 3 = 6

4 + 3 = 7

4 + 4 = 8

5 + 4 = 9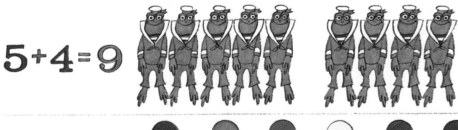

5 + 5 = 10